# THE SPACE BETWEEN WALLS

R.J. Romero

CittyKitty Enterprises

This book is a work of fiction. Names, characters,
places and incidents either are the product of the
author's imagination or are used fictitiously, and any
resemblance to actual persons, living or dead,
businesses, companies, events or locales is entirely
coincidental.

First Edition: November 2016
ebook: 978-0-9982616-0-7
printed: 978-0-9982616-1-4
Publisher: CittyKitty Enterprises, San Francisco, CA
Book and Cover design by R.J. Romero

For information contact :

http://www.rjromero.com
http://www.romeroartstudio.com/

# Dedication

This book is dedicated to my beloved husband, without whose corporeal support this book would have remained a specter haunting my dreams.

# CONTENTS

Within my breast a terror swells
as the occult darkness falls.
The unknown stalks the night and dwells
in the space between the walls.
--R.J. Romero

# CHAPTER 1
# YOUNG BRIDE

The great stone bastion that is Croftwood Castle has stood defiantly for over a hundred years, and will doubtless stand a hundred more. With its granite foundations, double-laid bricks, reinforced floors, and dual walls, that monstrous hulk could well withstand the battering of scorching heat, raging storm or decrepit time.

The countenance of almost any house is meant to inspire feelings of comfort under the sun's beam. As if to be contrary, the enormous manor house was an odious edifice of cold gray stone hewn into cruel lines meeting sharp angles, serving only to inspire dread in all who looked upon it. Even the trees and shrubbery that flourished on the estate maintained a cautious distance, much the same as the villagers. A great cacophony of gothic towers, crenelated walls, and myriad brick chimneys reared an arrogant head against the cloudy skies that glowered over the moor it stood upon. It had been devised thus by its owner, Howard R. Croftwood, a self-made industrialist seeking to tweak the nose of humanity in triumph of his success.

As others who have sprung from exceedingly humble beginnings, the master of the manor was an ambitious social-climber who sought desperately to purchase or emulate the trappings of the aristocracy. After investing the better part of his 57 years in building his fortune, he lavished much of it on creating a lasting monument to himself. What greater symbol of success and nobility could he wield than his own castle? So it was to this desolate fortress that the old pinchpenny eventually brought his most prized acquisition: a young bride.

By late afternoon the entire house staff had turned out, standing in rapt attention just outside the main entryway. The pretentious carriage had scarcely stopped before the brutish heavy frame of Croftwood lumbered out upon the gravel, barking at a footman to assist the remaining passenger, as he strode toward the front entrance.

The anxious footman dutifully lowered the collapsible steps from beneath the carriage frame. Holding the door wide, he held out a supportive arm. From the dim interior emerged a small gloved hand coming to rest upon his, then a young lady stepped out lightly from the carriage. At first the wide hat brim shadowed her face, until she looked up at the house, revealing two large hazel eyes set in a delicate pale oval face framed by long auburn ringlets. Attired in an ornate green velvet dress, the lady's hourglass figure and ample bosom gave mute testimony as to why the old reprobate had married her.

She was the loveliest woman Charles had ever seen. He would not have bothered coming out to watch the master's return from London, had he not been roused from his repose by the clamor of the preparations that had been going on all day. Looking at the beautiful young woman, a distinct arousal of another kind flared through him; something he had not felt in a great many years.

As each of the household employees was introduced to the mistress of Croftwood, the ladies curtsied and men bowed. The formidable housekeeper, Mrs. Gibbons, was cordial, belying a disapproving raised eyebrow over stern eyes.

The new mistress stopped to gaze across the rather bleak landscape, then back up at the cold gray façade of her domain, with an almost triumphant expression. Gathering up her skirts, she glided elegantly up the steps, entering into the great hall.

*** 

The new mistress looked around the great hall with wonder. In the windowless gloom, the many oil lamps and candelabras struggled against the dark cavernous expanse. The rough-hewn stone walls were hung with large tapestries and paintings, giving the hall a medieval quality. Directly across from the front entrance was a marble staircase with elaborately carved wood railings leading upward to a main landing where it branched off to opposite wings of the mansion.

"I never imagined it would be so grand," said the wide-eyed young lady. She removed her hat and gloves, handing them to the housekeeper.

"I'm glad you are pleased, madam," said Mrs. Gibbons proudly.

"Please call me Maude," the new mistress offered.

"That would not be proper, Mrs. Croftwood," said the housekeeper respectfully. "I expect you'd like a cup of tea after your journey."

Nodding for the mistress to follow, she walked ahead into the drawing room.

The tall French doors that led out to the terrace allowed a flood of light into the large richly decorated space. Again, the young woman was awed by the beauty and scale of the room. It seemed no detail had been overlooked in the choosing of rich fabrics, paintings, porcelain, and elegant furnishings from all over the world.

The ornate silver tea service was already prepared, along with an assortment of cakes and biscuits. Maude sat down carefully on the silk-covered divan. Mrs. Gibbons poured a cup of tea, then looked up at her expectantly.

"Oh, just a dash of cream please," she requested pleasantly. Accepting the cup of tea, she looked around at the wealth that surrounded her, trying to not show her unease at becoming the mistress of this huge manor house.

"If you would like to change any of the decorations, Mrs. Croftwood, you have but to tell me and I will attend to it."

"Thank you, Mrs. Gibbons. Although I can't imagine that I would change anything, but I will let you know."

Maude sipped delicately at the china teacup, shooting nervous glances at Mrs. Gibbons. Attired in a widow's customary black dress with a high collar, the thin middle-aged housekeeper looked drab and grim beyond her years. Indeed, it was almost as if she was an organic extension of the great manor itself; cold and tough as the very stone work.

"I'll have the maid bring in some lamps. It will be dark soon."

"It's not the dark I'm afraid of," Maude muttered to herself, glancing sideways at the housekeeper.

"Afraid?" Mrs. Gibbons asked suspiciously.

"Oh, pay me no mind. I suppose I was a little afraid that I wouldn't like it here," Maude offered as an explanation.

Mrs. Gibbons narrowed her eyes. She forced a polite smile as she glided toward the door.

"After all," Maude continued. "One hears such dreadful stories about these old houses—all dark and full of ghosts."

Mrs. Gibbons abruptly stopped. After a moment's pause for thought, she turned her head slightly over her shoulder. "I trust you will find your accommodations suitable. The chamber maid will be in shortly to show you to your rooms." Closing the door behind her, the housekeeper left Maude alone to finish her tea.

Despite the rich furnishings and fresh flowers, there was a cold gray gloom over the room, over the whole house. Laying down the teacup, Maude got up and stood looking out of the French doors, gazing past the terrace to the distant moors. Suddenly she felt a chill and very lonely. It wasn't only the isolation of being in a strange new environment. It was more as though she were an intruder here. The intimidating housekeeper, the old master of Croftwood, the desolate moor, and even the sullen sky seemed to belong to the cold formidable manor house.

Maude shook her head, dismissing the uneasiness, for to acknowledge such feelings would be to acknowledge fear. After finally attaining the wealth and station in life she had always wanted, albeit through a loveless marriage to a much older man, there was no turning back. She had always been a survivor. Come what may, there was no room for fear in her life.

A maid came in to the room with two large oil lamps which she placed on the table. Introducing herself as Janet, she offered to show the mistress to her rooms.

"Thank you, dear," Maud said cheerily, following the maid into the main hall. "I'm sure we'll become great friends, Janet."

The light in the drawing room faded to a dull red as evening crawled nearer to the mansion.

\*\*\*

As mistress of the house, Maude had been settled in what was intended to be the grandest bed chamber of the house, although the stone walls, heavy tapestries and dense velvet drapes produced a somber heaviness in the room. The large room was illuminated solely by three silver candelabras, casting shadowy fingers into the recesses of the room. The air was stale, heavy with the scent of burning wax candles.

The young mistress sat at the dressing table, gazing at herself in the large gilded mirror that hung above it. With a silver-plated brush, she gently stroked her long auburn hair which seemed to combust as it glimmered in the candle light.

Perhaps it was the unfamiliar surroundings, the chill of the stone walls or the nerves of a new bride, but Maude could not shake a gnawing uneasy feeling. The dim light of the candles flickered about the room, casting animated shadows.

At first she thought it was just a trick of the light that reflected off the mirror, creating a shadowy outline behind her, along with a peculiar awareness of someone being in the room. Thinking that her husband had come in without hearing him, she turned to greet him. The room was quite empty. Maude shrugged, flicking the brush through her hair and tried to dismiss the nervousness that prickled up her spine. Still, the uncomfortable sensation of a presence at her back lingered.

Abruptly, the lady stopped as if startled. Whirling round, she looked about the room searchingly until, satisfied at finding nothing, returned to task. Turning again to the mirror, she stared at the reflection of the chamber behind her with a look of bewilderment. Maude arose, walking around the room as if intending to discover something or someone.

Just then there was a sharp rhythmic rap on her door. The lady composed herself and bade the visitor to enter. It was Croftwood, bedecked in a vulgar crimson robe tied precariously around his girth. Without a word of greeting, he shuffled in on worn monogrammed leather slippers. As he leaned over to kiss the young woman, she turned and pointed toward the mirror.

"Is there anything the matter, my pet?" he asked cordially. "Do you not like your accommodations?"

"No, there was—," she began, wringing her hands nervously. "I thought there was someone in the room."

"You mean one of the male servants was in your room?" he demanded.

"No, no. It was—," she stammered again, then quickly changed her tone. "Oh, never you mind, dear. It must be the wine and I imagined it."

"Ah, so it was," he replied, confirming his wife's conclusion. "Now, how about givin' a little sweet to your new husband?"

He leaned into her, pressing chubby jowls into her delicate face. The young woman fidgeted to find a comfortable position, ultimately yielding to his clumsy advances.

The older man led her to the four-posted bed, leaving no doubt as to his intent as he clumsily fumbled to remove her night gown. Raising a gentle hand to coax his patience, the young woman finished disrobing. Croftwood's eyes guzzled the sight of the naked young body on the bed. He threw off his robe, revealing a naked thick hairy body that was clearly aroused. Then his fleshly bulk overtook her, the bedframe creaking in protest.

Suddenly, a low wail echoed against the stone walls. The couple's gyrations were halted by the lady sitting bolt upright in bed.

"Did you hear that?" she exclaimed.

"It's nothing, my pet," her husband purred reassuringly, annoyed at the interruption. "It's just the wind in the chimney. It happens this time of year."

His great bear paw of a hand pushed the reluctant young woman back down on the bed, determined to consummate his carnal ambitions. The old man's dreadful moans and bestial grunts added to the oppressive atmosphere of the room. Maude's face was ashen, devoid of expression, not that Croftwood would have noticed nor cared.

# Chapter 2
# The Apparition

The sun had all but finished its daily toil, yet Charles remained in that snug space between dreams and wakefulness to await the commotion of the household to settle. As evening approached, Charles decided to go see the beautiful lady again. In fact, he found himself quite unable to stay away.

The young mistress was seated before the mirror of her dressing table. From a large wooden box she drew out jeweled necklaces and earrings, holding them up against her soft pale skin, one after another. A look of intense pleasure lit up her features.

Obscured by a patch of deep shadow, Charles felt quite wicked to intrude on the lady's privacy. Yet, he was quite mesmerized watching her graceful movements. The lady's flowery perfume masked the odor of burning wax candles.

Admiring a rather gaudy emerald and gold lavalier, unexpectedly, the young woman stopped. Staring into the mirror, her hazel eyes became wide as saucers. The lady turned fearfully.

"Is someone there?" she demanded. "Come out into the light where I can see you!"

Charles froze, unsure of what to do. On no other occasion had anyone perceived his presence when he chose to peer out at the world, so he was rather lost for words to explain himself. He moved slowly into the aura of candle light, so as not to frighten her further.

"Who are you?" Maude asked, startled at his appearance.

"I'm sorry if I frightened you, m'lady," Charles said softly, in a consoling whisper. "Please—please, do not be afraid. I mean you no harm."

"Who are you?" she insisted. "And what do you mean by coming into my bedchamber?"

"Well, my name is Charles—Charles Watts," he mumbled uneasily. "That is, it was once."

"What do you mean 'it was once'?" she asked uneasily. For a moment, the alarmed young woman stared at him before realizing his meaning. A gasp escaped her lips.

Although Charles stood in the light, his form was semi-transparent, like a fog, revealing the chamber behind him. The sight of the pallid apparition chilled Maude into stone, unable to scream or to run.

"I'm dreadful sorry if I caused you a fright," he said soothingly, seeing her terror.

Finding the nerve to speak, she stammered, "Are you a *ghost*?"

"Well, yes, I suppose I do qualify on that score."

"What do you want with me?" she asked nervously.

"Why, nothing, m'lady," he reassured.

"Then why are you here? Why were you watching me?"

"Uh, well," he stammered awkwardly. "Didn't mean no harm—didn't mean for anyone to see me, least of all you. It's just...that is...well..." The ghost's voice cracked, as he stared down at the floor in embarrassment. "I've never seen a woman as beautiful like your ladyship."

The ghost's nervous manner seemed to ease Maude's fear somewhat, whilst still unsure of what peril it represented. Nevertheless, the curious young lady arose and guardedly came closer, examining the ghostly figure. Like an inquisitive child, with a cautious gesture she poked a finger forward into his chest, only to have her whole hand pass through. Again the lady shrank back fearfully. Maude shrank back to the dressing table, hastily putting away her jewels while eyeing the apparition suspiciously.

In the large gilded mirror Charles caught sight of his own shadowy figure that vaguely resembled the man he once had been. It was a shock, since he had not beheld his spectral form in many years. His once handsome features had decayed into an emaciated cadaverous wraith, albeit not entirely inhuman. The familiar reflection still wore the same work clothes as when he had drawn his final breath. He was greatly distressed that this was the impression that the new Mistress of the house had of him. It was no wonder that she was afraid and repelled.

Upon locking the large wooden jewel case, Maude turned to face him, leaning a lovely pink arm on the back of the satin covered chair.

"You were here last night, weren't you?" she accused. "I saw you in the mirror."

"Well, yes," he mumbled apologetically. "I'm awful sorry about that. Didn't mean any harm."

"No *harm*? It means you must have seen me—well, *undressed*!" she said indignantly, sitting down again. "I've never heard of a Peeping Tom ghost, although I should not be surprised, given that you were once a man," she added sternly.

Deep guilt swept through Charles, much like when his mother scolded him for a childish transgression. He deeply regretted having caused the lady any disquiet. Whilst the ghost had thought that he could not be seen by mortals, somehow the candlelight and mirror had betrayed his presence. Then again, Charles didn't really know how things were supposed to work for a disembodied spirit. Despite his present condition, all he knew about ghosts was what he'd heard in his youth.

"Was that you who moaned last night?"

"Yes, I'm afraid so," the ghost said ashamedly. "I never intended to—it just sort of came out of me. I just couldn't bear to see how Croftwood dishonored you."

As if in agreement with his comment, a slight smile curled the ends of her full lips. She gazed at the ghost thoughtfully, evaluating the unearthly intruder.

"Well, Mr. Watts, since it would seem we are now on rather intimate terms, you may call me Maude."

"Pleased to make your acquaintance," he replied, bowing awkwardly. Never having been schooled in proper manners or how to behave with ladies, it was more a fear of being thought an ignorant peasant than etiquette dictating that he should behave respectfully.

"I certainly never expected to make the acquaintance of a ghost," she said thoughtfully.

"Truth be told, m'lady, I never expected to be one."

They both laughed at his ironic remark, which served to put them both at ease. Maude was truly beautiful when she laughed, Charles thought.

"It's rather curious, even as a little girl I have never been afraid of the dark. But then one hears such horrid things about ghosts. Should I not be afraid of you?"

"No, m'lady, I swear on my honor that you have nothing to fear from me," the spirit assured her. "I'm just a hapless soul that would rather be your friend."

"Well now, Mr. Watts, that would really be quite something—being friends with a ghost," she mused, a slight thrill sparking her mind. Maude began to consider the implications and possibilities of such an unusual camaraderie.

"If it pleases your ladyship, I would very much like that as well."

"Are there any other spirits in this house that I should be concerned about?" She asked cautiously.

"None that I've ever seen since this manor was built."

"Good, I am glad to hear it," Maude replied in a relieved tone. "As I am new to this part of the country, it would certainly be nice to have a friend in this house."

"Indeed," Charles agreed eagerly. "I have not had the pleasure of a lady's friendship in a very long time."

"Well, I am sure we shall have sufficient time to get acquainted; however, the hour is now late, and my husband may be coming to call. Would you be so kind as to leave me?"

"Yes, ma'am," he replied, instinctively bowing.

Maude laughed, amused by his awkward manners. "I'm not the queen, you know." Those pretty hazel eyes kept laughing at him, but it did not matter to Charles. It had been countless years since he was a young man in the company of a charming young lady.

"Before you leave, Charles, I would like your word, as a gentleman, that you will not visit or spy on me when I am—well, *indisposed*."

"No, ma'am—that is—yes, I promise." If the ghost could have blushed in embarrassment, he surely would have. "I shall keep to myself and call only at a suitable hour, if it pleases your ladyship."

Apparently satisfied at this, Maude returned to the mirror to begin the nightly ritual of brushing her luxuriant hair.

After one last glance, Charles retreated back into the deep shadows where he dwelt. As he sank into slumber, the image of the lady's silken auburn hair in the candle light warmed his soul. Whilst the recent years had been filled with loneliness, or rather a kind of nothingness, it was comforting to discover that an incorporeal spirit was still capable of feeling happiness.

# CHAPTER 3
# AN UNTIMELY
# DEATH

Over the ensuing weeks, routine became the order of the day for the mistress of the manor. Maude threw herself into her new role, attending to matters of the household, exploring the gloomy expanse of the manor or taking long walks to inspect the grounds. With a casual friendly manner and quick wit, she quickly endeared herself to most of the staff. Mrs. Gibbons, who easily found fault with everyone, thought the new Mrs. Croftwood was someone 'common' from the big city, trying to act like gentry in the country.

While not a natural outdoorsman, Mr. Croftwood endeavored to pursue the same activities enjoyed by titled gentry. When not out riding or shooting, he immersed himself in business affairs each day, taking scarce notice of his attractive young wife's presence until they sat at meals or upon visiting her bedchamber.

Croftwood had always felt that privileged society looked down upon his sort, due to his humble origins and coarse manner. This made him doggedly focused on building his fortune, rather than cultivating the appropriate contacts or manners needed to rise in polite society. So it was that he led a mostly solitary life, save for a handful of business associates he might share a pint with when he was in London.

In time Charles and Maude established a routine of evening visits at their appointed hour, as would a gentleman call on a lady, despite the disparity of him being a resurrected spirit. As the weeks passed, a distinct transformation had come over Charles. His countenance had returned to more closely resemble the pleasant looking fellow he had been when he lived. He also found that in brighter light, the more solid his form appeared which made him look less inhuman.

During their evening visits, the two discussed many topics, but he most enjoyed stories about Maude's early life growing up in London, finding success on the music hall stage, in addition to what it was like to live in the greatest metropolis of the world. It was always sad for him when their visit came to an end, especially when interrupted by Croftwood's familiar brusque knock. Charles had come to treasure Maude's company, while attempting to ignore that she was married to the loathsome master of the manor.

\*\*\*

A violent autumn storm was creeping over the country side; cannons of thunder rumbled as icy rain pelted the brooding stone manor house. Flashes of lightning silhouetted its gothic spires and towers into great black talons scratching at the raging clouds.

When the ghost came to call, Maude was not in her usual talkative mood. The bedchamber's candlelight struggled weakly against the gloom, creating shadows that were impenetrable black voids. But it was not the roaring onslaught of the storm or the shadowy gloom that dampened the lady's spirits.

"I'm afraid I'm not much in the mood for conversation," Maude said sadly.

"Is it the storm? Are you not well?" Charles inquired politely.

"I am well enough," she replied glumly. "The storm's chill is nothing to what my life has become."

"I'm sorry, I do not understand."

"It's just that my marriage—well, things don't always turn out as happily as we think it will be."

"Is he unkind to you?" the ghost asked, concerned for her happiness. Charles had no doubt that Croftwood treated her badly.

"Oh, pay me no heed. Perhaps it is the storm breeding melancholy," she replied. Changing the subject, Maude straightened up in her chair, attempting a smile. "Enough about me. Indeed, I have told you much about myself, yet you remain a mystery to me. I would much rather learn more about you."

"My life has been a short and simple one," he explained, uncomfortable to speak of himself. "There is not much left to tell that I have not already."

"Ah, but you have not yet told me how it was you came to haunt this house."

"That is something I had hoped you would not ask me," he replied sadly. Charles stared down at the carpet broodingly.

"But as your friend, I would very much like to know what happened to you," she urged.

Abruptly, a red glow appeared in the core of the ghost's figure, lighting his stern face from beneath. His glaring eyes glowed with reddish light.

"It is because of your *wretched husband* that I am condemned to walk these halls!" Charles snarled angrily.

Although startled at his outburst, Maude did not register much reaction at all. A look of confusion knitted her brow.

"Are you trying to say that my husband was the cause of your death?" she asked in a surprised tone.

"Aye, and I am damned for it!"

Rather than being upset, Maude was intrigued. Leaning on the right arm of the satin chair, she supported her face with her thumb and forefinger.

"Pray, do go on," she requested gently.

\*\*\*

THE GHOST RELATES HIS STORY.

Sometimes I find that I have forgotten things from years gone by, but that one day reverberates within the psychic chambers of my memory. It was over twenty years ago, when this house was being built. Croftwood was much younger then, having become a very wealthy man by his mid-thirties. Construction of the manor was to be accomplished in only three years, due to his relentless oversight to cut costs. He lavished his fortune on the materials, bringing in stones and exotic woods from distant places, which were carved by the best craftsmen of the time. Yet, he wasn't so generous with the local village workmen. He bullied, harassed and cheated them until they abandoned the construction altogether, forcing him to replace them with imported laborers from the surrounding counties. I was one of those workers who came to build these very walls.

It was a cold late afternoon in October, when most of the work was done for the day. I was completing some work on the top floor. Most of the men had already left for the village pub for dinner. Croftwood made it his practice to inspect each day's work, so I was trying to finish setting one of the beams. Somehow, my ladder slipped, and I fell over sideways. Being that I was of a thin build, I became lodged between the double walls, scarcely able to move. I yelled for my mate, who had been nearby; however, it was Croftwood's face I saw looking down at me.

He called down, "You there, are you injured?"

"Can't really say, sir," I replied. "Seems I'm stuck tight in here."

After a few minutes, he dropped a rope down to pull me out. So I grabbed hold of it tight with both hands, best as I could. Although he pulled hard I was lodged in too tight in that narrow space.

"I'm awful sorry to be so much trouble, sir," I called up to him. "We'll need more help to get me out."

"Everyone's gone to the village," he said in an irritated voice.

"I'd be much obliged if you'd get a couple of the lads to come help." I requested, as nice as I could. "They may have to break through the walls to get me out."

Even though the evening sky was getting dark, I could see his face glaring at me in the faint light. Then he said: "That'll cost me hundreds of pounds! Am I supposed to rip up these walls just because a clumsy lout gets himself stuck?"

His face disappeared. Even though he was angry, I supposed that he had gone to find help, like any Christian man would. The next thing I knew, particles of dirt fell on my face. Then it was followed by more, as shovelfuls of gravel and earth came down on me. I thought the structure above me was beginning to crumble. I tried to yell for help, but the falling dust got into my mouth, forcing me to keep it closed. When the falling debris stopped, I realized that if I did not free myself soon, I would be *buried alive*!

I didn't see nor hear Croftwood again. Surely, he would return soon with some of the lads to get me out, or so I thought. The night's chill drifted down the shaft of my lonely prison as the hours passed.

In desperation I twisted and bucked against the rubble atop me, the weight of it thwarting my efforts. A profound need to scream clawed at my fraying mind. I opened my mouth, but nothing came out. My chest was pressed tight between the walls, so it was difficult to get enough air in my lungs just to breathe. With the dust grating at my dry throat, my fading gasps were lost to the cold indifferent night. At length, overtaken by exhaustion, I fell into a profound dreamless sleep.

When I regained consciousness, it was daylight again. I could hear the pounding and voices of the men working above me. Then the horrible realization hit me: it was Croftwood who shoveled the rubble on top of me. That bastard had left me here to die!

My rage, as well as the threat of an agonizing death, lashed me into action. I writhed about, scratching and pushing, to force the dirt off me that I might alert the men to my location. But it was all to no avail, since I was too weak and there being too much debris on top of me.

Then the panic of impending suffocation flooded my mind, instinctively generating an effort to scream. My parched lips and tongue moved convulsively in the attempt, but no voice came forth from my lungs, which were oppressed as if by the weight of a mountain, struggling for every labored breath. I desperately gasped to harvest the last remnants of air against the dry dust filling my nose, mouth and lungs. You cannot imagine the horror of suffocating slowly... your lungs aching with each rasping breath... leading ever closer to the last. Your mind is aware that you are dying with each passing minute, yet still it fights against the certain doom that you will soon cease to exist.

Too weak to move further, I wondered if just giving in and dying would prove a better escape than fighting to prolong this agony. Mercifully, my mind grew numb as the gray semi-consciousness turned into a black oblivion.

Despite my mother's insistence on a Christian upbringing, I had never held any strong beliefs in Heaven or Hell. It turned out I ended up in neither place. For some unknown period, I drifted in a black silent void of nothingness, like a dreamless half-sleep. At last, there arrived a time in which I found myself emerging into the first vague sense of existence again. Just as the day dawns upon a weary traveler who has journeyed through a long desolate night, so too the light of my soul seemed to come back to me.

All at once, I found myself standing in the main hall of this very manor, which had now been completed. There were servants walking about, yet no one paid any attention to me as I passed by them. Like awakening from a nightmare, my mind tried to regain its grasp on reality with countless questions. Was I still alive? Had I been rescued? Or was it all just a horrible dream?

All at once I was shocked into stone. Paralyzed with fear, I stood staring at the mirror that hangs in the entrance hall. In front of me was the terrifying corpselike reflection of a dead man! Instinctively, I looked down at my hands, and I could see the floor right through them! Never having seen such a ghostly vision, it frightened me to my core to realize that the monster before me was me! Can you imagine the absurdity of a ghost being afraid of itself?

Of course I came to realize that I was indeed dead, the woeful acceptance seeping into my soul. Because I had died without a Christian burial, I reasoned, as long as my bones lay in unconsecrated ground I was doomed to haunt this damnable house. A great melancholy overcame me, so I hid myself away in the shadows, not knowing if I would ever see Heaven, Hell or remain in this Purgatory until the end of days.

\*\*\*

The ghost finished his story, staring dejectedly down at the carpet. It had been unexpectedly painful for him to recount—indeed, relive—his agonizing death and subsequent resurrection of so many years ago. The red glow of anger had dissipated, as many emotions stirred in him that heretofore had been forgotten.

The heaviness of his voice, the gravity of every word, seemed too serious for Maude to doubt the veracity of his story or find words of comfort to offer.

"Charles, I am so sorry," Maude said gently. "I don't know quite what to say."

"There is nothing more to be said on the matter. I apologize for my outburst and ending our visit on such a somber tone."

Bidding her a good evening, the ghost's form passed through the wall into the darkness beyond.

Still stunned by the Charles' story, Maude turned her chair toward the dressing table, staring pensively into the mirror. She had been greatly moved by Charles' tale, which gave her a different perception of her husband, in turn sparking new thoughts about her future.

# CHAPTER 4
# DINNER FOR THREE

The flickering candle light from the crystal chandelier hanging in the center of the ceiling cast dancing shadows over the great dining hall. A cheery fire in the grate of the carved oak fireplace provided much needed warmth against the damp cold that penetrated the stone walls.

While the master and mistress sat at opposite ends of the long dinner table in silence, the house staff served each course and removed the delicate china dishes dutifully. An arrangement of fresh-cut wild flowers in the center of the table barely allowed the couple to see each other, if they cared to. Having served the meat course, the servants retreated from the room, allowing the couple their privacy. There was hardly a need for privacy, as there was never much conversation between the married couple, at meals or any other time. The lack of companionship or affection from her husband left Maude feeling lonely and isolated.

Croftwood greedily devoured his dinner of roasted lamb and potatoes, barely pausing to wash it down with gulps of wine, while his wife watched with restrained disgust. Picking at her meal listlessly, out of boredom Maude decided to break the awkward silence.

"How was your day?" she asked gently. "I hardly ever see you."

"See me? What the devil do you need to see me for?" answered Croftwood gruffly. "You should have everything you need, don't you?"

"Well, you needn't be so surly. Why shouldn't a wife want the company of her husband?"

Croftwood looked up, surprised at her comment. His usual gruff expression softened momentarily as he regarded his lovely young wife from across the table. The beautiful russet haired mistress of the manor was fetchingly clad in a dark green velvet gown with a low neckline and exposed shoulders. Her diamond and emerald jewelry sparkled like stars in the candle light, illuminating her face. A twinge of unfamiliar emotion pricked his heart. Then, as if waking from a dream, he sadly lowered his eyes back to his meal.

"Mrs. Gibbons tells me you've been ordering new draperies and some things for the house," Croftwood said in an accusatory manor.

"Why, yes, I thought some changes would make our home a bit more cheery and elegant."

"Elegant, eh? Well, don't you go spending my money like you're the bloody queen," he grumbled.

"No, dear," responded Maude dismissively.

In a shadowy corner of the room behind Croftwood, Charles stood motionless, watching them. Noticing his presence, Maude was surprised to see him, yet strangely comforted. The ghost raised a finger to his lips as if to indicate his manifestation was their secret, as Charles had explained to her that when he willed it his spirit could remain invisible to those he did not wish to see him.

Then an irresistible mischievous urge prompted Maude to engage her husband in more conversation.

"By the way, dear, you never told me that we had a ghost in this house," she said innocently.

"What? A ghost?" sputtered a startled Croftwood. He nearly choked on a mouthful of food, which he managed to swallow. "What nonsense is this?"

Maude could see Charles smiling, enjoying her making sport of his enemy. The spirit floated closer to the table to get a better view of Croftwood's expression.

"It's just that I heard a story that a man that was killed when they were building this manor. They say his spirit still haunts this place."

"I don't know what you're talking about," her husband grumbled impatiently. "You shouldn't believe such foolish local gossip."

"That is why I'm asking you, dear, since I am a stranger here and don't know what happened years ago."

"Well, have you seen a ghost?" Croftwood asked uneasily.

"Why no, not as yet," Maude answered coyly.

"There you are then. Anyway, there's no such thing as ghosts," he said dismissively, eager to change the subject.

As Croftwood reached for his wine goblet, suddenly it moved and tipped over, pushed by Charles' unseen hand, spilling its blood red contents over the table and onto Croftwood's lap. The old man cried out in surprise, quickly mopping up the wine from his clothing with a napkin.

Maude broke out into a hearty laugh. Smiling like a impish boy, Charles winked at her before disappearing into the shadows.

"Maybe it was the ghost of Croftwood Castle," she suggested, giggling mischievously.

"Don't you dare laugh!" Croftwood growled angrily. "Don't you *ever* laugh at me!" His face contorted into a mask of rage Maude had never seen before.

Bolting to his feet, the rasp of his chair on the wood floor sounded like a shriek of pain. In four paces the stocky Croftwood quickly crossed the length of the table to where his startled wife sat. He thrust his large hands around her slender pale throat, raising a wide-eyed Maude up out of her chair. The frightened woman grasped his wrists desperately, trying to gain some ease from the deadly grip that threatened to choke her.

"Don't you ever laugh at me, you little guttersnipe!" he threatened. Croftwood pressed his angry intense eyes close to hers. "Remember you are my wife—I own you until death us do part!"

Then he released her neck, pushing his gasping wife back against the chair. The color drained from her face as a primal instinct for survival gripped her heart, her frightened eyes watching him cautiously.

Just as abruptly as his outburst, Croftwood's expression transformed from anger to a sneer, then to something more ominous as his gaze fell below Maude's frightened face. His squinted eyes took in the soft pink glow of her exposed skin. Reaching out with one hand he grasped her waist, bringing his wife close to him, while the other hand roamed greedily over the young woman's full bosom.

"Prepare yourself, madam, I shall be visiting your bed chamber presently," he warned, raising one bushy eyebrow haughtily.

Croftwood turned on his heel and stomped out of the room, almost triumphantly. A shaken Maude regarded her husband's retreating figure from narrowed thoughtful eyes.

"Till death us do part," she repeated under her breath. The fright caused by Croftwood's sudden assault faded into a strange numbness. Now was not the time to try to resolve the situation.

Quickly fixing her hair and straightening her dress, Maude rang for the servants to have them clear the table. As mistress of the manor, keeping up an appearance that all was well was what was expected of her—no matter what happened. Maude forced a stoic smile and bid the servants a hasty 'good night' before rushing upstairs, lest the servants notice her distress.

***

The bed chamber seemed colder than usual, despite a robust fire in the grate. Maude sat dejectedly in front of her dressing table, a raging torrent of anger, desperation, and helplessness flooding her mind. What she had hoped would be a pleasant marriage of convenience with Croftwood had become intolerable, especially since discovering he was responsible for Charles' death. But before seeking any resolution to her marital situation, Maude would need to steel herself to endure another night of her husband's visits.

She had scarcely taken her hair down to brush it before a familiar rattle of the door latch caused her to start. Without the usual courteous knock, her husband barged into the bedchamber, slamming the door behind him. The reflection of Maude's face in the ornate mirror became a hardened blank stare, watching the corpulent figure of Croftwood approaching her.

# CHAPTER 5
# DEADLY BARGAIN

The following night Charles found Maude draped over the dressing table, her upper torso heaving as she cried into her handkerchief. Having never seen a woman so distressed, the ghost was unsure how to comfort her, yet he was concerned for her wellbeing.

"Maude, I am here. Why are you weeping?"

The young woman raised her tear-streaked face. Despite looking tired, she was no less beautiful to him.

"Oh, Charles," she said sadly. "I'm sorry to have you see me this way. It's just...I just cannot bear it any longer."

"What is it, Maude? What's happened?"

"It is him—it is always him."

"Croftwood? What has he done?"

"You have seen the way he treats me during the day: cold and indifferent. But you have no idea what happens at night when he comes to call. I dread each sunset, knowing that it means he may come to my bedchamber."

"Well, I cannot blame you if you do not wish to lie with that contemptable old rogue," he said uneasily. "Yet, I suppose, he is still your husband."

"That is easy for you to say because you are a man," she said tearfully. "You do not understand. It is not the normal love making of a husband and wife. I could abide that well enough, as any wife must. But he makes me do vile, unspeakable things that decent folk have never dreamt of. He treats me no better than a trollop." She turned away, again weeping.

Although outrage riled him, Charles was unsure how to react to this sordid revelation. He felt powerless being not much more than a shadow; a mere semblance of a man. Moreover, these were sensitive matters between a married couple, with which he had no experience.

"Maude, I—" he began hesitantly, unsure of what to say.

"Dear Charles, I know there's nothing you can do to help me," she moaned. "I value your friendship, but there is no one who can help me now. I must take matters into my own hands."

"What do you mean?" he asked, becoming alarmed.

"I simply cannot bear the thought of another night with his great paws all over me or what he may force upon me," she said gravely.

"Do you mean you intend to leave Croftwood?"

"I cannot leave him without being ruined socially," she replied despondently. "Before you came tonight, I was contemplating hurling myself off the highest tower of this wretched mausoleum!"

The shock of her words shot through Charles like a bolt of lightning. He had never known anyone who had wanted to destroy themselves. Both the Catholic and Protestant churches taught that suicide was a mortal sin, which would condemn her soul to Hell. The very thought of Maude's soul being damned—as he was now damned to walk the earth—was horrifying to him.

"No, Maude," he pleaded. "You must never do such a thing!"

"You don't know what it's like. I am his prisoner here, beyond hope or caring."

"There must be another way that you can be set free," Charles insisted. "Surely he will not live much longer."

"His doctors told him that his heart is weak, so he must avoid any great shock at all costs. Still, with proper care, he can live a very long life indeed." Maude dabbed at her tears with a silk handkerchief, watching the ghost's reaction. "Yet, I can no longer bear to live with his depravity. Only death can release me now. If not his, then it must be mine."

The solution seemed obvious, although Charles was reluctant to accept it. The thought of Croftwood meeting a ghastly death had crossed his mind several times before, but never had the ghost thought of killing the scoundrel himself. He did not even know if he possessed any supernatural powers that he could employ for such a purpose. Nonetheless, he could not bear to see Maude so despondent, nor the thought of her suicide for the sake of the man who had murdered him.

"Do not distress yourself any further," he declared solemnly. "I will rid you of this monster."

Sobbing gently, Maude turned toward him, her large hazel eyes regarding him sadly before asking, "But what can you do? You are but a ghost."

"Aye, a ghost—a ghost that can frighten the bloody bastard to an early grave!"

At this, Maude's face brightened, until a look of cautious apprehension overtook it. She stood and looked up at Charles, wringing her hands nervously.

"I—I cannot ask this of you," she cried. "I dare not. It would be murder. My soul would be damned."

"You will be innocent of any wrong-doing, my dear. I can no longer avoid confronting the villain who condemned me to this living nightmare."

"I cannot fault you for avenging yourself upon my husband," said Maude, looking directly into his eyes. "If you do so, I promise that I shall tear the walls of this house down until I find your bones, and give them a Christian burial so that you may find eternal peace."

Her promise touched him deeply. Whilst he did not wish to be parted from Maude, the prospect of being granted final rest was more than he had hoped for these past lonely years.

"I will choose a time and place for what must be done," the ghost said. "However, you must promise me that you will do nothing to harm yourself."

"Yes, I promise," she said solemnly. "You have given me hope again, for which I cannot thank you enough."

The ghost took his leave from Maude, gazing longingly at her face, made porcelain in the candle light, as he disappeared into the gloomy dark recesses behind the walls. He wanted to take her up in his arms and protect her forever, although he knew it could never be.

While he did not have a particularly strong belief in God, especially in his present state, Charles considered that perhaps this was part of some divine plan that was laid before him. Here was an opportunity to avenge his own murder, as well as save Maude's soul from a fate truly worse than death. A growing anger and thirst for vengeance fueled a fiery red glow that lit the ghost's shape from within his very core.

# Chapter 6
# Fires of Rage

A cheerless fire smoldered impotently in the stone fireplace of the library, leaving a damp chill in the air. The room was wide with high ceilings; its walls on three sides were lined with fully stocked bookshelves. Several pewter candelabras were strategically placed around the room, yet only the one atop the desk was frugally lit. Blending into the deep shadows, the ghost watched the master of Croftwood sorting through papers at his medieval desk. The thought of Maude being pawed and mistreated by this ogre hardened his resolve; his growing anger manifesting in an aura of fiery red light around the specter's shape.

Croftwood looked up suspiciously, and called out: "Is someone there?" He scanned the dimly lit room until he detected a red glow outlining the mysterious figure of a man in the shadows. "Who are you?" the old man demanded. "Stop hiding in the shadows like a coward."

"I am no coward," said Charles defiantly, stepping out into the candle light. "I am the man you sentenced to a living death. It is time to pay for your crimes!"

"What nonsense is this," said the old man dubiously. "Who are you and how did you get in here?" The master of the manor rose in a defensive stance.

"Charles Watts was my name, not that you cared to know it," the ghost said accusingly.

A look of astonishment transformed the aged gentleman's face. His memory was not as good as it had once been, yet he recognized the young workman that had once interrupted the construction of his castle.

"That was many years ago. You are supposed to be dead," he said incredulously. Straining his skeptical eyes in the hazy light, his hand instinctively reached for the small dagger he kept on the desk to open his letters.

"Indeed, sir, I am dead, because of you. You left me to suffer an agonizing death, condemning my soul with no Christian burial to give me peace."

"So, what do you want? Money, I suppose?"

"Money cannot redeem a murderer," the ghost sneered.

A look of anger distorted the master's timeworn features as he came around the desk to confront the mysterious visitor. Whilst age mellows the hearts of most men, Croftwood was no less malevolent than he had ever been.

"I don't know what kind of trick this is, but you, sir, are a thief and a liar—not a ghost!"

With a sudden thrust, Croftwood's hand holding the dagger penetrated the space of the specter's chest, passing through to the wall. Shocked at what he saw, the old man stumbled backward against the desk in disbelief, his mouth agape.

"You—you *are* a ghost!" He gasped, his small eyes rounding into bulging globes. The old man stared in horrified disbelief at the cadaverous wraith before him.

"Tell me what I may do to make things right?" Croftwood pleaded. He clutched at his chest, pangs of guilt and fear clawing at his racing heart.

"You cannot make right a willful murder," Charles snapped. The vicious attack by Croftwood had further fueled his outrage. "My spirit is condemned forever to haunt these halls because of you."

"What do you intend to do with me?" Croftwood stammered.

"You must be punished for what you have done," the ghost declared.

"Why now after so many years?

"You have committed many offences in your lifetime, no less than murder in my case," replied the angry ghost. "But I can stand by no longer to watch your abuse and mistreatment of the lady."

"The lady? What lady?" Croftwood asked, struggling to comprehend. "Do you mean Maude? But she is my wife. What bloody business is it of yours what I do with her?"

"She may be your wife, but she deserves far better than the sordid likes of you."

The ghost's words sparked a wicked realization in the crafty old man's mind. Narrowing his eyes suspiciously, Croftwood said, "So it would seem a ghost is in love with my wife." Arrogance, along with an innate sense of survival, began to thaw the chill of fear. "And what would you have me do? Divorce the lady?" he asked scornfully.

"You know full well that would ruin her reputation in decent society."

"Well then, perhaps you plan to murder me, then 'spirit' the wealthy widow away?" The old rascal asked sarcastically.

"It would not be murder—it would be justice!" the ghost threatened.

"I would bargain with you, ghost," Croftwood offered. "You may have the girl to do with as you please, in exchange for my safety."

"I will not make such a treacherous bargain with the likes of you," growled Charles, incensed.

"No, I suppose a ripe experienced woman like Maude would not be of much use to a ghost," the sly reprobate said mockingly.

Becoming increasingly agitated, the specter warned: "You should not speak of the lady in such a manner." The anger that had been growing in him had now developed into a bright fiery glow that lit his spectral form from within.

"Ah, perhaps you don't know the lady as well as I do," Croftwood replied teasingly. "I met Maudie in one of the more disreputable music halls in London. She was more woman than I had ever met before. In my own way I came to care for her, I suppose; her charms quite bewitched me. But make no mistake, sir, our marriage is one of mutual convenience. Our union was a business transaction: my money for her favors. So, in the end, that *lady* is no better than any other tart." The old scoundrel snickered maliciously; his expression was one of impassive scorn.

Charles had never before felt such hatred toward any living being as he did at that moment. The sensation of raw fury surged through him, feeding upon itself to more intensity. A blazing red light encircled the ghost, as he moved closer toward the defiant Croftwood. Then the apparition arose, floating upward, expanding in breadth and height. A roaring whirlwind swept the room, as tufts of flames shot from the ghost's eyes and fingers, swirling around and through him, transforming into a hideous demon from the molten depths of Hell itself! Fiery claws reached out toward the old man.

Croftwood screamed in terror at the hellish vision swirling over him. Falling to his knees, he clutched his chest with one hand, raising the other defensively. That old wicked heart beat ever faster in stabbing fear, thumping spasmodically, until his exhausted body collapsed, wracked in the final throes of death. The realization of dying with his unforgiven sins clawed at Croftwood's final thoughts. A call for help smothered on his lips as his body went still. Then an eerie silence saturated the room.

The fiery yellow eyes of the demon scrutinized the lifeless body before it to ensure Croftwood was dead. With his rage subsiding, the hellish apparition gradually returned to the semblance of Charles' earthly form. He was pleased to know that by being a disembodied spirit he was capable of such great fury and power.

Charles' face was innocent of human feeling, as he gazed indifferently at the feeble pathetic figure crumpled on the carpet. Like so many arrogant wealthy men, Croftwood had thought he was beyond the chain of cause and effect. The cruel and corrupt things he had done ... the laws he had ignored ... the troubles he had caused others ... the mistreatment of Maude ... his death was a justifiable fate that the old rogue had brought upon himself. Thusly, the ghost justified Croftwood's death as he dissolved back into the shadows.

Their master's screams had roused some of the staff, who knocked and called to him from behind the study door. It was the butler who took it upon himself to enter the room, only to discover Croftwood's lifeless remains twisted in a final agony, his rounded eyes bulging in terror.

# CHAPTER 7
# THE FALL

As AS THE ONLY TWO ATTENDEES from the manor house, the housekeeper and butler related to the maids how the funeral had been a dismal sparsely-attended affair held in the village chapel. Of great note was the scandalous absence of the widow, although the Anglican priest sited extreme grief to excuse her nonattendance.

"I've never seen the like," Mrs. Gibbons said indignantly. "It's appalling behavior to not attend her own husband's funeral just because she's too busy packing to go to London." The female staff nodded their agreement, assuming expressions of disapproval.

The butler added, "That reminds me, the carriage should be 'round in a few minutes."

"I'll go tell her ladyship," offered the chambermaid.

"Don't call her that!" snapped the housekeeper. "That woman is not a lady!"

The maid cupped a hand over her mouth to shade a mischievous snicker, before rushing off toward the main staircase.

\*\*\*

"Thank you, Janet," Maude said hurriedly to the maid. "Tell the coachman he may load up the trunk and bags. I will be down directly."

"Yes, Mrs. Croftwood," said the maid obediently as she turned to leave the room.

Charles lurked in the shadows watching the new widow primping in the gilded mirror over the dressing table. Maude carefully powdered her face, applied rouge, and fussed with her elaborate gown. The dark crimson fabric of the bodice was overlaid with black lace embroidered with shiny black beads, over a deep red taffeta skirt that had a shadow of black threads woven through it. In her mind, the garish costume was an appropriate compromise for the traditional widow's weeds.

"Where are you going?" Charles asked in a low sad voice.

"Oh! You startled me," she replied, as if annoyed at the interruption. "I'm leaving."

"For how long?"

"Forever, if I have anything to do with it," she murmured under her breath.

"You did not tell me that you would be leaving. I thought we were friends."

"Of course we are, luv. I truly appreciate what you did for me. Really I do," Maude said solicitously, yet a tone of insincerity undermined her words.

"You didn't even go to his funeral."

"Well, I've been so busy with all this packin'," she explained. "The old gent's death was terrible, of course, but I need to get on with my life. I'm sure you're glad he got what was comin' to him."

"Yes, I hated him for what he did to me, but I despised him even more for how he mistreated you."

"You wanted him dead just as much as I did," she accused.

"No, I only did it for you—because you talked about doing away with yourself. I couldn't bear the thought of your soul being damned—like mine—because of him."

"Yes, that was a bit of good actin', wasn't it?" she stated proudly. "Back in my music hall days, I was the best actress they had. That's where I met the old gent. He said I was the best he'd ever seen, though it wasn't my talent he was after."

Maude was acting very differently now, no longer feeling obliged to maintain a lady-like demeanor. The ghost stared blankly at her, not knowing what to make of this transformation. Had his feelings for her blinded him to what she really was?

"I was afraid I'd have to wait years for the old goat to drop dead. I couldn't very well push him down the stairs now could I? They'd have suspected the young wife straight off. But if his old heart gave out, nobody would think twice about the poor grievin' widow."

The shock of her admission was like the cold slap of winter on the first snowfall. Realization of Maude's true nature and intentions roiled inside his very soul.

"You just used me!" Charles shouted angrily. "Croftwood tried to tell me, but I wouldn't listen. You're nothing but a—."

"Now, now, luv, no need to take on so," Maude countered. "We both got what we wanted, eh? You got your revenge and I'm free as a bird." She happily flapped her graceful hands theatrically. "A very *rich* bird!"

"So you're just going to leave me here?" the ghost asked, realizing she had no regard for him. In all of his lonely years as a spirit, Charles had never felt so desolate as that moment; like an abandoned lover.

"What? Did you think I was going to stay in this old mausoleum living happily ever after with a *ghost*?" she said sarcastically. Maude admired her reflection in the mirror one last time, turning herself to ensure that the lavish skirts of her dress looked presentable.

"Life is for the livin', dearie, and I've got a lot of livin' left to do."

"But you promised to find my bones and give them a Christian burial," pleaded the ghost.

"Oh, yes, I suppose I did. Well, don't fret, luv. You may stay on here as long as you like. After all, I might need your services again someday," she said flippantly. Walking toward the chamber door, Maude slipped on black lace gloves over her slender pale hands. She turned back toward Charles with a callous smile curling her rosebud lips. "After all, it's always nice to have a man around the house to help with the unpleasant chores."

Suddenly, the heavy wooden door of the room was assailed by a loud pounding, like the fist of a giant seeking entrance. At first startled, Maude hurled a suspicious look at Charles.

"Now, don't try any of your ghost tricks with me. You can't scare me into stayin'. I'm glad to get away from you and this cursed place!"

Opening the bed chamber door, Maude froze in mid-exit. Her beautiful hazel eyes grew even larger in astonishment. There in the hallway was the ghostly figure of Howard Croftwood! His semi-transparent form hovered just slightly above the carpet with an angry red light glowing from within him.

"Hello, my pet. How about a little sweet for your husband?" he snarled. The unearthly sound was a low raspy version of that voice Charles had hoped to never hear again.

Although still recognizable, the decayed yellowish skin of Croftwood's face was drawn tight against his skull, leaving his eyes bulging out of deep black sockets. His dried pale lips twisted into a menacing grimace.

"No! It's not possible," Maude stammered, shaking her head in denial. There was genuine terror in her eyes as she staggered back into the corridor. "You're—you're dead!"

"Oh yes, my dear. *Dead* but clearly not departed. Did you think you'd be rid of me so easily?"

Shocked and confused, Charles watched helplessly as the vaporous figure of Croftwood floated nearer to the horrified Maude. Clearly, a Christian burial was no guarantee of eternal rest if a spirit was somehow disturbed or riled enough to seek vengeance.

"Our business is not yet done, my beloved wife," growled Croftwood, his spectral glowing fingers reached out for her menacingly.

Maude stared wide-eyed, raising her hands defensively. Then the walls echoed with her throat-wrenching high-pitched scream.

Spinning round on her heels, the terrified Maude ran desperately for the landing at the top of the stairs. Reaching for the banister, her gloved hand slipped on the smooth polished wood, the voluminous skirts of her dress twisting around her legs, causing her to fall forward onto the marble stairs. Another loud shriek briefly escaped her lips until a stone stair tread snapped her neck. The dreadful sounds of her fragile body being pummeled and broken marked the violent descent.

The crashing tumult roused the servants, who quickly abandoned their tasks to investigate. Amidst screams and alarmed shouting, the staff rushed about in leaderless chaos. Finally comprehending there was naught to be done, they gathered silently, aghast at what lay before them. At the terminus of that precipitous fall lay the bloodied shattered corpse of their mistress, with a look of fear in her dead staring eyes.

As the household staff looked at each other in slack-jawed bewilderment, the walls echoed with the unmistakable laughter of the dead master of Croftwood Castle.

# THE SPACE BETWEEN WALLS

# Epilogue

Croftwood Castle may yet stand a hundred years more with its brick chimneys and gothic spires piercing the forlorn sky. Nonetheless, the natural wild of the land gradually began to reclaim its due upon the resources stolen from it.

In the ensuing years following that lady's untimely end, the great manor house was shut up, shunned by humankind and vermin alike. The only existent Croftwood heir spent but a fortnight before making a hasty departure, refusing to inhabit the cursed place. Nor has any willing buyer to be found since.

Whilst deserted by all, the great stone leviathan pines not in lonely solitude, for there remain three inhabitants that wander its silent dark corridors, forever tormented with a history of greed and murder. They still dwell in the space between walls.

# THE SPACE BETWEEN WALLS

# About the Author

R.J. Romero is the pen name for Rita Romero, an independent author living her creative dreams in San Francisco. She writes in a wide range that includes poetry, horror, and other stories that blur the boundary between reality and possibility.

When not writing, Rita Romero is also an award winning visual artist. The unique combination of being both a writer and a painter infuses her literary work with an uncommon artistic approach to conjure vivid images that lend both literal and symbolic meanings to her writing.

For more information on other books by R.J. Romero visit: http://www.rjromero.com

# Books by R.J. Romero

If you enjoyed reading this book, check out these other works available at amazon.com or wherever you like to shop for books.

The Space Between Walls

An Untimely Frost

Dark Reflections